Then it Rained

written by Crystal J. Stranaghan
illustrated by Rosa Espadaler

gumboot books
www.gumbootbooks.ca

This **book** belongs
in the **library** of

_____

_____

_____

Note for Librarians:
A cataloguing record for this book is available from
Library and Archives Canada at
www.collectionscanada.ca/amicus/index-e.html

ISBN 978-0-9784047-8-9 (hardcover)
ISBN 142511452-0 (softcover)

This book proudly printed and bound in Canada,
by Friesens Corporation.

Other Gumboot Books titles by Crystal J. Stranaghan:

Vernon and the Snake (2007)
ill. Eleanor Rosenberg

The 13th Floor: Primed for Adventure (2007)
ill. Izabela Bzymek

Faeries Are Real (2007)
ill. Izabela Bzymek

For my family, who showed me
how to dream big and work hard,

and for Jared and Jen,
who held my hands while I jumped.

C.J.S.

For my supportive family,
and my insightful teacher Maja.

R.E.

T he weatherman
promised a sky free of grey,
so we planned a great picnic for our class
field trip day.

With hours and hours before it got dark,
we'd play hundreds of games and eat lunch in
the park.

We cheered when we got there and the teachers
explained, our assignment today was
"Have fun"...

...then it **rained**!

First **one** drop,

then **two** drops,

then **three**,

and then **four**,

and then **five hundred thousand and forty-five** more!

"Oh No!" cried the teachers.

"We can't **picnic** in **that.** We'll be **drenched** to the skin in just **two** seconds **flat!**"

We got **back** on the **bus,** all packed in cheek to **cheek.**

Our **picnic** put off until **"maybe next week".**

When the **weekend** arrived and the weather had **changed,** it was **baseball** we wanted, the game all **arranged.**

We did **sit-ups** and **push-ups** and **stretches** galore,

and made **piles** of **all** of our **gear** by the **door.**

It was **cloudy** but **dry** as
we set up the **game.**

The first **batter**
stepped up to the **plate...**

...then it rained!

First **one** drop,

then **two** drops,

then **three**,

and then **four**,

and then seventeen
million and ninety-two more!

"**Oh no!**" cried the coaches, "We **can't** play in **that!** We'll get mud on our **gloves** and the **ball** and the **bat!**"

So we **jumped** in our vans and drove **home** through the **rain,** where we sat **watching** baseball on TV, **again.**

Monday and **Tuesday** and **Wednesday** were **fair**.

So was **Thursday** I saw from my **school desk** and **chair**.

Although **Friday** was **cloudy**, the weatherman **promised**, come **Saturday** there would be **sunshine**: No, Honest!

We packed **towels** and **buckets** and **lunch** and we strained to get **all** of our stuff to the **beach**...

...then it **rained!**

First **one** drop, then **two** drops,

then **three**, and then **four**,

and then six billion three hundred thousand four more!

"Oh no!" cried the parents. **"quick** back to the **car.** Thank **goodness** the parking lot's not **very** far!"

Our **whole weekend** passed by,
noses **pressed** to the pane,
as we **watched** out the **window**
for sunshine, **in vain!**

I **yelled** to my dad,
sister, brother and **mom:**

"I am **tired** of waiting for what
might not come! I was **four,**
and then **five,** pretty soon I'll be
seven. I'm **not** staying inside
until I'm **eleven**!

I'm **bored** and I'm
grumpy all cooped
up **again,** just
because of a really
quite small
bit of **rain."**

"Why **can't** I get **wet?**

What will
happen to **me?**

Don't I get
soaking wet
when I **swim**
in the **sea?**

My **skin** has
seen **water** at
bathtime,
I know,

and in **wintertime** after I **play** in the **snow.**

I'm **sure** we have **raincoats** and **hats** for a **reason...**

...and when **should** we wear them if not **rainy** season?"

"Oh No!" cried the grownups in **horrified** voices. **"Surely** there must be some much **better** choices. Ones that **do not** involve **muddy** or **wet.** Should we tell you **again** just how **sick** you might **get?"**

"I suppose that I **might**, but might's **no guarantee.**

Can't I bundle up **warmly** and **try it** and **see?**

Please - **please**, pretty **please** with a **cherry** on top?

Because **isn't** it **possible** this **rain** might **not stop?**

I'm **not** scared of **mud** or a **small** bit of **wet**, and there's just **so** much **fun** that I **haven't** had **yet!**"

"We suppose" said the grownups,
who had somehow forgotten that when they were
young there were days that were rotten.

When getting all muddy and wet was
a game, and they hadn't yet learned
to be scared of the rain.

So on went our boots, and with hearts
loudly thumping, outside we all went
to go mud puddle jumping!

First **one** splash,

then **two** splashes,

then **three**,

and then **four**,

and then **no one** was **scared** of the **rain anymore!**